MR. TALL

by Roger Hargreaves

Mr Tall was very very very tall.

Quite the tallest person you've ever met.

In fact, quite the tallest person you've never met, because you've never met anybody with legs as long as Mr Tall's legs.

Have you?

Now, the problem with being as tall as Mr Tall,
meant that life was just one long problem.

As you can see!

"Oh dear," he used to sigh.

"Oh dear me! I do so wish that my legs weren't quite so very very very long."

He decided to go for a walk to think over his problem.

He was just stepping over a tree when he heard a voice.

A little voice.

"Hello!"

It was Mr Small, standing underneath a daisy.

But Mr Tall was so tall he couldn't see him.

So Mr Small shouted at the top of his voice.

"Hello!"

A Mr Small shout is about as loud as a bee's sneeze.

So, it took quite some time for Mr Tall to spot him.

"Oh," he said gloomily. "It's you."

"You don't look very happy," said Mr Small. "What's up?"

"I am," replied Mr Tall. "Because of these silly long legs of mine."

"Oh," said Mr Small.

Mr Small decided to cheer him up.

"Let's go for a walk together," he suggested.

So they did, which of course didn't work.

It was like a giraffe going for a walk with a mouse!

Then Mr Small had an idea.

Which did work!

And, because of the length of Mr Tall's legs, they very quickly walked all the way to the seaside.

"Come for a swim," cried Mr Small.

"Can't," replied Mr Tall. "By the time it gets deep enough for me to swim I'll be out the other side."

So Mr Small went for a swim, while Mr Tall sat down with a face which was nearly as long as his legs.

Mr Tickle came along.

"Hello," he said. "You look as if you need cheering up. Care for a tickle?"

"No thanks," replied Mr Tall. "What I would care for are some different legs. Mine are much too long."

"So are my arms," said Mr Tickle cheerfully. "But all the better for tickling!"

And off he went, chuckling, looking for somebody to tickle.

Looking for anybody to tickle!

Mr Nosey came along.

"Cheer up," he said. "You look very down in the mouth. What's the problem?"

"It's my legs," replied Mr Tall. "They're too long!"

"So's my nose," replied Mr Nosey, laughing. "But all the better for poking into other people's business!"

And he went off, looking for something to be nosey about.

Looking for anything to be nosey about.

Mr Greedy came along.

"Hello," he cried. "You look gloomy! What's wrong?"

"It's my legs," explained Mr Tall. "They're too big!"

"So is my tummy," replied Mr Greedy. "But all the better for filling with food!"

And off he went, licking his lips.

Mr Tall sat there and thought about Mr Tickle's arms, and Mr Nosey's nose, and Mr Greedy's tummy.

He smiled.

And then, he grinned.

And then he laughed out loud.

He looked at his legs, those very very very long legs of his.

"All the better for walking," he chuckled.

And walked home.

In four minutes.

Forty miles!

Mr Small came out of the sea after his short swim.

"And how am I going to get home?" he asked himself.

So, he set off walking.

All the way home.

Forty miles!

That was last year.

He got home yesterday!

Fantastic offers for Mr. Men fans!

Collect all your Mr. Men or Little Miss books in these superb durable collectors' cases!

Only £5.99 inc. postage and packing, these wipe-clean, hard-wearing cases will give all your Mr. Men or Little Miss books a beautiful new home!

Keep track of your collection with this giant-sized double-sided Mr. Men and Little Miss Collectors' poster.

Collect 6 tokens and we will send you a brilliant giant-sized double-sided collectors' poster! Simply tape a £1 coin to cover postage and packaging in the space provided and fill out the form overleaf.

STICK £1 COIN HERE (for poster only)

Only need a few Mr. Men or Little Miss to complete your set? You can order any of the titles on the back of the books from our Mr. Men order line on 0870 787 1724. Orders should be delivered between 5 and 7 working days.

--- **TO BE COMPLETED BY AN ADULT** ---

To apply for any of these great offers, ask an adult to complete the details below and send this whole page with the appropriate payment and tokens, to: MR. MEN CLASSIC OFFER, PO BOX 715, HORSHAM RH12 5WG

☐ Please send me a giant-sized double-sided collectors' poster.
AND ☐ I enclose 6 tokens and have taped a £1 coin to the other side of this page.

☐ Please send me ☐ Mr. Men Library case(s) and/or ☐ Little Miss library case(s) at £5.99 each inc P&P

☐ I enclose a cheque/postal order payable to Egmont UK Limited for £...............

OR ☐ Please debit my MasterCard / Visa / Maestro / Delta account (delete as appropriate) for £...............

Card no. ☐☐☐☐ ☐☐☐☐ ☐☐☐☐ ☐☐☐☐ ☐☐☐☐   Security code ☐☐☐

Issue no. (if available) ☐   Start Date ☐☐/☐☐/☐☐   Expiry Date ☐☐/☐☐/☐☐

Fan's name: ....   Date of birth: ....

Address: ....

....

Postcode: ....

Name of parent / guardian: ....

Email for parent / guardian: ....

Signature of parent / guardian: ....

Please allow 28 days for delivery. Offer is only available while stocks last. We reserve the right to change the terms of this offer at any time and we offer a 14 day money back guarantee. This does not affect your statutory rights. Offers apply to UK only.

☐ We may occasionally wish to send you information about other Egmont children's books.
If you would rather we didn't, please tick this box.

Ref: MRM 001